For my sister Soudade, who helped bring this book into existence. Thank you for coming on this journey with me and for being my creative partner in crime!

And for Mama Atouf, who presented me with my first paint set at the age of eight, even when the shop seller kept saying, "It's for professional artists not children!" You answered, "Well, that's what she'll be one day..."

**Nadine**

Published in the United Kingdom in 2018 by Lantana Publishing Ltd., London
www.lantanapublishing.com

American edition published in 2018 by Lantana Publishing Ltd., UK
info@lantanapublishing.com

Translated from Arabic. Originally published in 2012 by Box of Tales Publishing House, Syria.

Text, Illustration & Translation © Nadine Kaadan 2018

Distributed in the United States and Canada by Lerner Publishing Group, Inc.
241 First Avenue North, Minneapolis, MN 55401 U.S.A.
For reading levels and more information, look for this title at www.lernerbooks.com
Cataloging-in-Publication Data Available

Printed and bound in Europe
Original art created with watercolor and pencils on paper

ISBN: 978-1-911373-43-8
eBook ISBN: 978-1-911373-46-9

# Tomorrow

### Nadine Kaadan

LANTANA
PUBLISHING

Yazan no longer went to the park, and he no longer saw his friend who lived next door.

Everything around him was changing.

Even his mother
had changed.
She had stopped
painting.

Yazan and his
mother used
to spend hours
painting together.

Sometimes, he
had been happy
just watching her
paint.

Now, the minute she woke up she would watch the news with the volume turned up loud...SO LOUD!

Each time they wanted to leave the house, Yazan's father would make lots of phone calls.

When Yazan asked why, he would say, "Traffic! We're trying to avoid the traffic."

Yazan felt really stuck: no park, and no friends. One day there was school, and then no school the next.

He even started to miss going to school, which was a surprise!

That weekend, the hours seemed so long with nothing to do.

Yazan got out of bed and tried to keep himself busy.

He drew a few doodles.

He built a castle out of pillows.

He even made 142 paper planes.

But he was
still BORED!

BORED!

BORED!

He went to the living room and screamed,
"I want to go to the park NOWWWWWWWW!!"

But his parents were watching the news and didn't
even turn around.

"Not today, Yazan," said his mother.

Yazan grabbed his bicycle, which he hadn't touched for over a month.

He stood by the front door and wondered whether to go to the park by himself.

He thought long and hard about it.

He knew his mother would be angry if he left without her permission. But he looked at his bike, and was tempted by its shiny red paint and its new bell that made four different sounds.

TINGALINGALING!

He opened the door and walked outside. When he reached the street, it was completely empty. Everything was different.

Abu Saeed, who sold tasty beans and cumin from his trolley, was nowhere to be seen. Neither were the kids Yazan usually played with. Frightening sounds exploded all around.

Yazan didn't know what to do. Should he continue to the park or go back home?

Suddenly he saw his father striding towards him. He took his hand and they walked home together.

Yazan waited to be told off for leaving the house without permission.

But his father didn't say a word.

When they arrived home, Yazan's mother was waiting for him.

She ran to him and hugged him very tightly. "Don't ever EVER go out of the house by yourself again!" she said.

She looked at Yazan and his little red bike. Then she grabbed her paintbrushes and paints, and went to Yazan's room.

"YAY! Mama is painting again!" Yazan cried.

His father smiled. "But this time she'll be painting on the wall."

Yazan sat and watched his mother painting on the wall of his bedroom.

"I'm really sorry," she said, "but you can't go to the park right now. People are fighting in the streets, and going out of the house is too dangerous."

"When will the fighting be over?" asked Yazan.

"I don't know," replied his mother. "But let's paint a park in your bedroom—an amazing park with everything you've ever dreamed of. And soon, you'll be able to go outside again and play."

Dear reader,

Have you ever been stuck in the house when you're desperate to go outside? Unfortunately for Yazan, like many children in Syria, this is the reality of war, forcing him to stay at home because the streets are too dangerous to play in.

I wrote this story because I saw children like Yazan in my hometown of Damascus. Their lives were changing, and they couldn't understand why. All of a sudden, the Fridays that were supposed to mark our weekends became frightening instead of fun. Families were afraid to go outside and instead stayed home.

I noticed that my illustration style started changing. Where once I was drawn to dreamy tones, my palette became gloomy and dark. I felt the need to express what was happening around me so I decided to write this book.

Almost a decade later, the situation continues to worsen for Syrian children, especially those who are living away from their homes and who have missed years of school. Today, we wait for a time when "tomorrow" can be a better day for all Syrian children.

Nadine